Color & Learn Easy FRENCH PHRASES FOR KIDS

Roz Fulcher

Salut.
sah-loo

Dover Publications, Inc.
Mineola, New York

This handy book will have you speaking French in no time! More than sixty illustrated pages include commonly used words and phrases in both French and English. Below each French word or phrase you'll find its pronunciation. Syllables in French have equal stress.

Whether it's just for fun, for travel, or to have a conversation with a friend or relative, you'll find out how to talk about the weather, tell what you'd like at mealtime, and many other helpful phrases—and you can color while you learn!

Bibliographical Note

Color & Learn Easy French Phrases for Kids is a new work, first published by Dover Publications, Inc., in 2015.

International Standard Book Number

ISBN-13: 978-0-486-80361-6
ISBN-10: 0-486-80361-9

Manufactured in the United States by LSC Communications
80361908   2020
www.doverpublications.com

Good morning.

Hello.   Good-bye.

See you later.

What's your name?

My name is _____.

Voici 1. *Ma mère*
Vwah see   mah mare

2. *Mon père*
    mone pare

3. *Ma soeur*
   ma sur

4. *Mon frère*
   mone frair

This is my   1. Mother   2. Father
              3. Sister   4. Brother

How old are you?   I am _____ years old.

I'm allergic to nuts/eggs.

I love you.

What's for breakfast? 1. Cereal

2. une tartine
oon tar-teen

3. des oeufs
day zuh

2. Toast

3. Eggs

It's time for lunch. I want. . . 1. a sandwich

2. un yaourt
uhn yah-oort

3. un hamburger
uhn ahn-boor-gur

2. Yogurt   3. Hamburger

I'm hungry! What's for dinner?

14

1. du poulet?
doo poo-lay

2. du poisson?
doo pwa-sone

3. de la pizza?
deuh la pih-zah

1. Chicken?   2. Fish?   3. Pizza?

What's for dessert?

1. de la glace
duh lah glahss

2. un fruit
uhn fwee

3. des biscuits
day biss-kwee

1. Ice cream   2. Fruit   3. Cookies

17

I like to . . . 1. Read 2. Dance

4. Faire de la bicyclette
fair duh la bee-see-clett

3. Dessiner
day-see-nay

3. Draw   4. Bike

1. I'm sorry.   2. Don't worry.
3. It's okay.

Can you help me, please? I'm lost.

Joyeux Noël!

zhwah-yuh no-ehl

Merry Christmas!

Bonne année!

bone ah-nay

Happy New Year!

This is delicious! I'd like some more.

Where are you from?   I am from _____.

Les jours de la semaine

Lay joor duh las suh-mehn

Monday ☀ *le lundi*
luh luhn-dee

Tuesday ☁ *le mardi*
luh marr-dee

Wednesday *le mercredi*
luh mair-kruh-dee

Days of the week

Thursday *le jeudi*
luh zhuh-dee

Friday *le vendredi*
luh vahn-druh-dee

Saturday *le samedi*
luh sahm-dee

Sunday *le dimanche*
luh dih-manzhe

Les mois
lay mwah

January	February	March
janvier	*fevrier*	*mars*
jahn-vee-ay	fay-vree-ay	marze

April	May	June
avril	*mai*	*juin*
vreel	may	zhwahn

Months

July
juillet
zhwee-ay

August
aout
ooh

September
septembre
say-tahn-bruh

October
octobre
ock-toe-bruh

November
novembre
noh-vahn-bruh

December
décembre
day-sahn-bruh

Les nombres
lay nohmb

un
uhn

deux
deuh

trois
twah

quatre
kat

cinq
sank

Numbers

six
seese

sept
set

huit
wheet

neuf
nerff

dix
deess

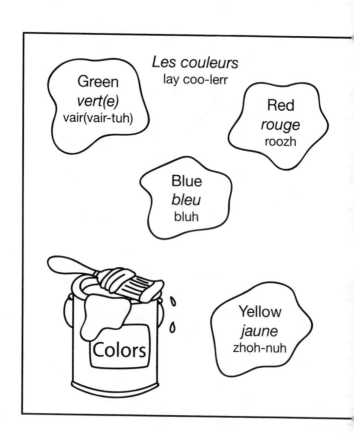

Les couleurs
lay coo-lerr

Green
vert(e)
vair(vair-tuh)

Red
rouge
roozh

Blue
bleu
bluh

Yellow
jaune
zhoh-nuh

Colors

Colors

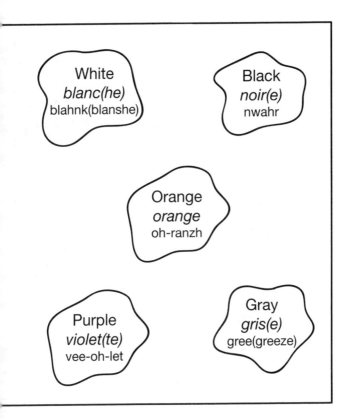

White
blanc(he)
blahnk(blanshe)

Black
noir(e)
nwahr

Orange
orange
oh-ranzh

Purple
violet(te)
vee-oh-let

Gray
gris(e)
gree(greeze)

33

1. Let's go to the park!
2. Awesome idea!

1. How much does it cost?

2. It's one dollar.

Let's go to the beach! I will get . . .

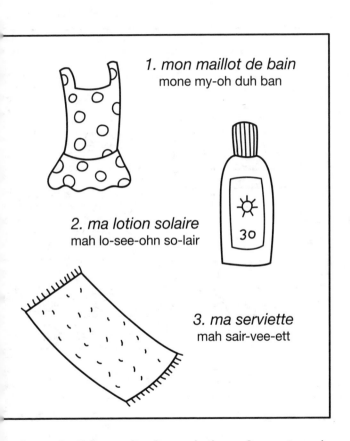

1. mon maillot de bain
mone my-oh duh ban

2. ma lotion solaire
mah lo-see-ohn so-lair

3. ma serviette
mah sair-vee-ett

1. my bathing suit   2. my lotion   3. my towel

Please.

Thank you.   You're welcome.

It's raining. I'm taking . . .
1. my umbrella   2. my raincoat

Could you speak more slowly?

It's hot today. I'll wear . . .

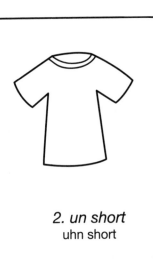

1. un t-shirt
uhn tee-shurt

2. un short
uhn short

3. des sandales
day sahn-doll

1. a T-shirt   2. shorts   3. sandals

It's snowing! I need . . .

1. mon écharpe
mone ay-sharp

2. mes gants
may gahn

3. mes bottes
may bah-tuh

4. mon manteaux
mone mahn-toe

1. my scarf   2. my gloves
3. my boots   4. my coat

I'm cold. I need . . .

1. un tricot
uhn tree-koe

2. une couverture
oon coo-vair-toor

3. une veste
oon vest

1. a sweater   2. a blanket   3. a jacket

Do you speak English?

Sorry, I don't understand.

I'm thirsty. I want . . .

1. *de l'eau*
duh low

2. *du jus*
doo zhoo

3. *du lait*
doo lay

1. water   2. juice   3. milk

Excuse me. Where is the nearest . . .

1. Restaurant?
ress-toe-rahn

2. Arrêt d'autobus?
ah-ray dau-toe-boos

3. Métro?
may-troh

1. restaurant?   2. bus stop?

3. subway?

Do you have a pet?   I have . . .

1. un chien
uhn shee-yen

2. un chat
uhn shah

3. un poisson
uhn pwah-son

4. un oiseau
uhn wha-zoh

5. un hamster
uhn am-stair

1. a dog   2. a cat   3. a fish

4. a bird   5. a hamster

Happy birthday! My birthday is in

_____.

Can I . . . 1. Watch TV?
2. Go to a movie?
3. Go outside?

Where is the bathroom?

1. *Grand-mère*
grahn-mayre

2. *Grand-père*
grahn-pair

3. *Tante*
Tahn-tuh

4. *Oncle*
Ohn-kluh

5. *Cousine*
Koo-zeen

6. *Cousin*
Koo-zan

1. Grandma
2. Grandpa
3. Aunt
4. Uncle
5. Cousin (girl)
6. Cousin (boy)

I don't feel well. My . . . 1. throat   2. head
3. stomach . . . (hurts)

60

I'm tired. Time for bed.

Good night.